Amelia's Fantastic Flight

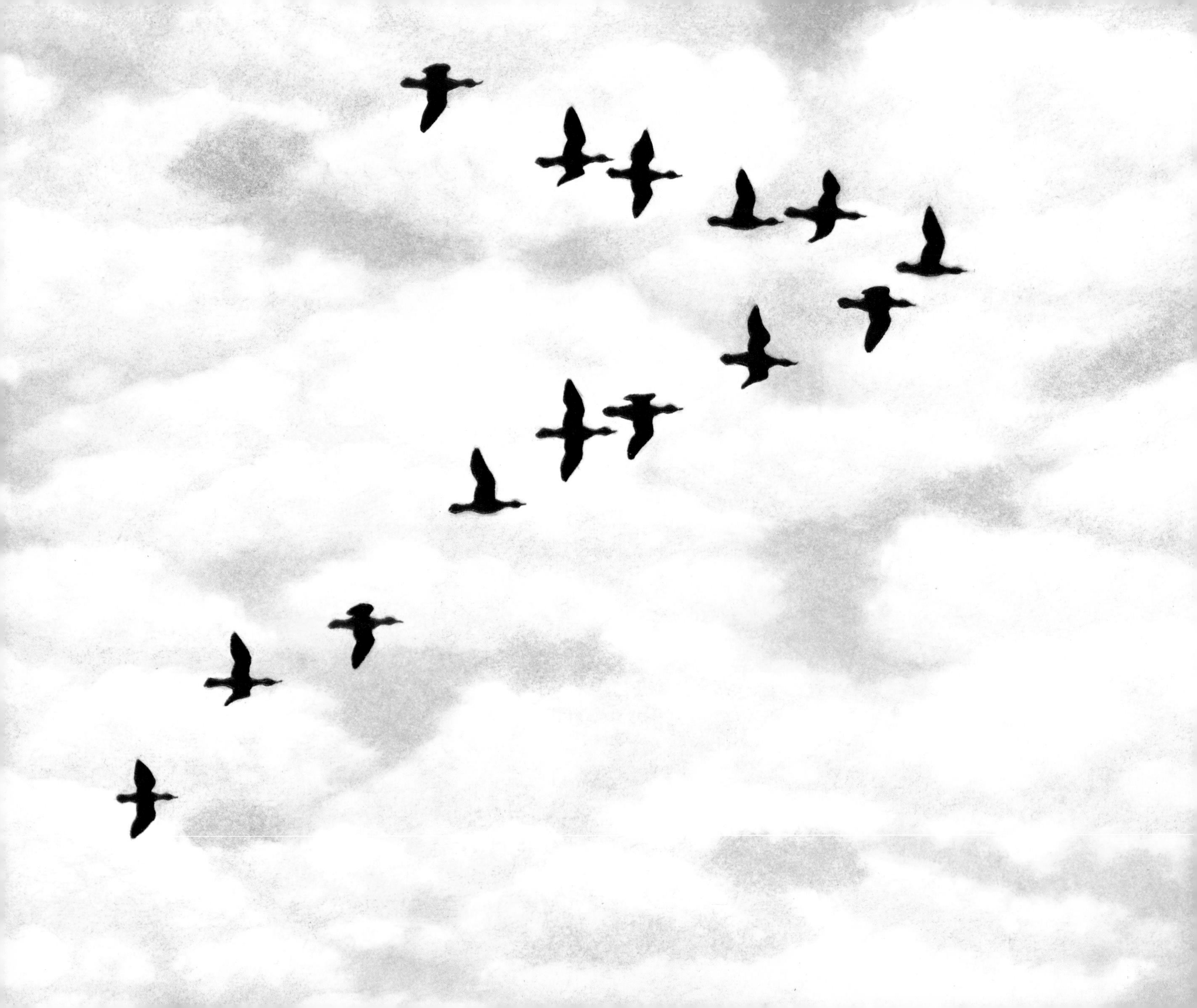

Amelia's Fantastic Flight

BY ROSE BURSIK

Henry Holt and Company ✦ New York

Published by Henry Holt and Company, Inc.,
115 West 18th Street, New York, New York 10011.
Published simultaneously in Canada
by Fitzhenry & Whiteside Ltd.,
195 Allstate Parkway, Markham, Ontario L3R 4T8.

Library of Congress Cataloging-in-Publication Data
Bursik, Rose.
Amelia's fantastic flight / by Rose Bursik.
Summary: A young girl builds her own airplane and flies around
the world, "freezing in Finland," "charmed by China," and getting
"a kick out of Kenya"—before returning home for dinner.
ISBN 0-8050-1872-7
[1. Airplanes—Fiction.   2. Voyages around the world—Fiction.
3. Imagination—Fiction.]   I. Title.
PZ77B94544Am   1992   [E]—dc20   91-28809

Henry Holt books are available at special discounts
for bulk purchases for sales promotions, premiums,
fund-raising, or educational use. Special editions
or book excerpts can also be created to specification.

Printed in the United States of America
on acid-free paper. ∞

10 9 8 7 6 5 4 3 2 1

to George and Teresa

Amelia loved airplanes.

So she built one.

And she took it...

...for a little spin.

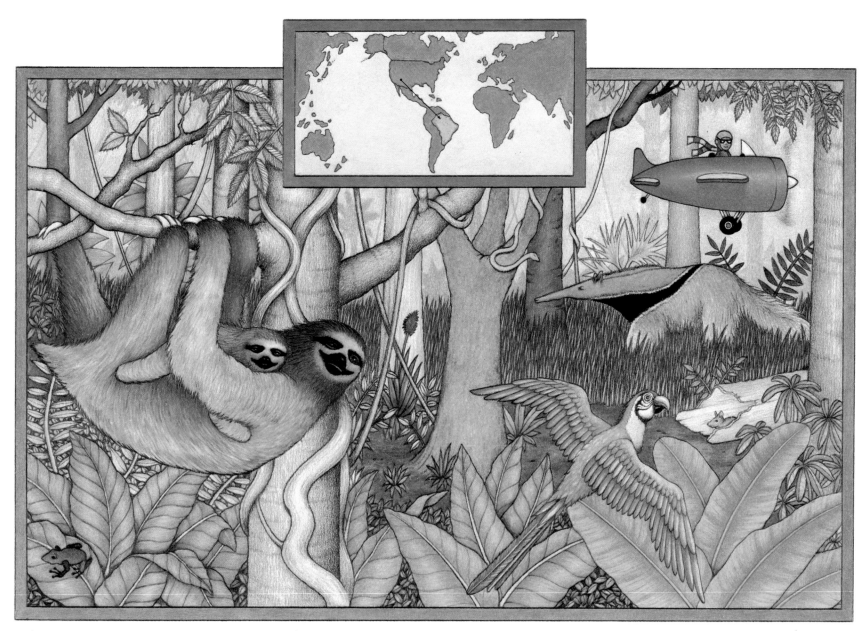

She breezed through Brazil,

and she got a kick out of Kenya.

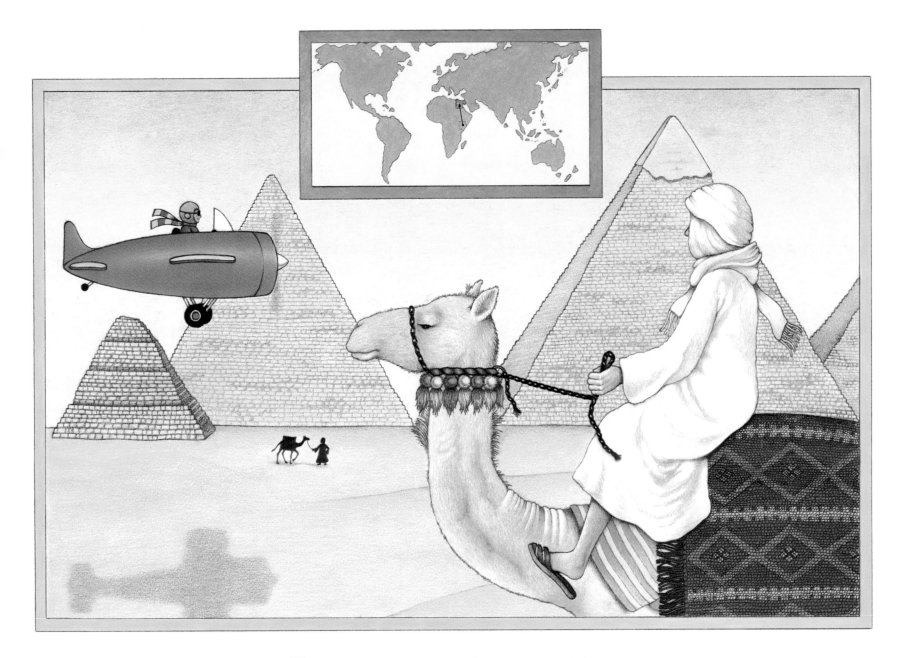

Egypt was entirely enjoyable,

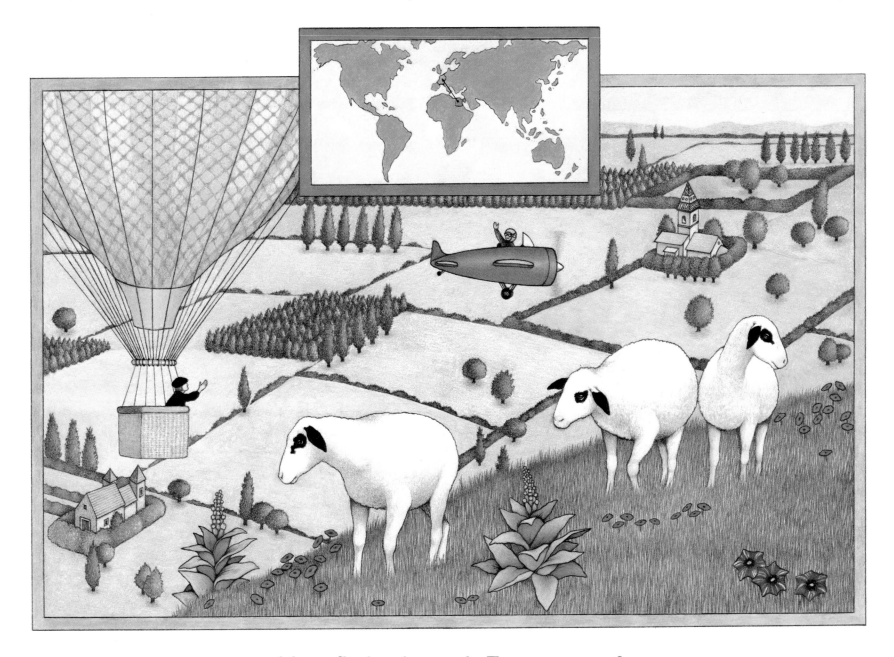

and her flight through France was fun.

After freezing in Finland,

she soared through the Soviet Union.

Though she found India interesting,

she napped in Nepal.

She was charmed by China,

and Japan was just a joy.

Australia was altogether amazing,

and she had a terrific time in Tahiti.

But she malfunctioned in Mexico!

After making a few quick repairs,

Amelia hurried back home.

And she landed just in time

...for dinner

...and a bedtime story.

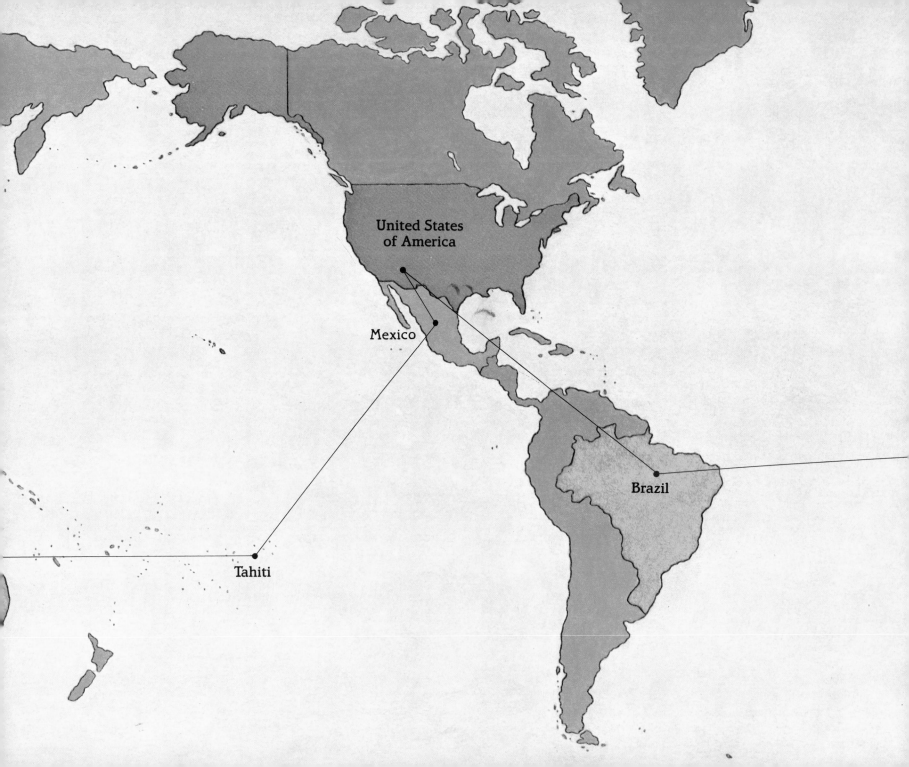

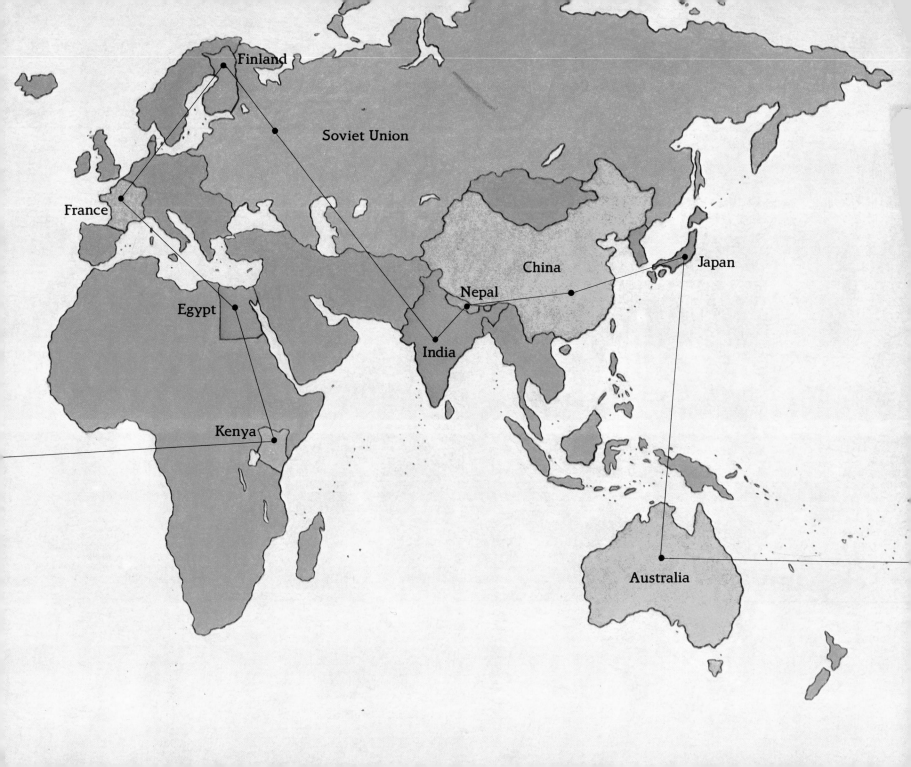